By Elise Allen

EGMONT

Meet the Faraway Fairies

Favourite Colour – Yellow. It's a beautiful colour that reminds me of sunshine and happiness.
Talent – Light. I can release rays of energy to light up a room or, if I really try hard, I can use it to break out of tight situations. The only problem is that when I lose my temper I can have a 'flash attack' which is really embarrassing because my friends find it funny.
Favourite Activity – Exploring. I love an adventure, even when it gets me into trouble. I never get tired of visiting new places and meeting new people.

Favourite Colour – Blue. The colour of the sea and the sky. I love every shade from aquamarine to midnight blue.
Talent – As well as being a musician I can also transform into other objects. I like to do it for fun, but it also comes in useful if there's a spot of bother.
Favourite Activity – Singing and dancing. I can do it all day and never get tired.

Favourite Colour – Green. It's the colour of life. All my best plant friends are one shade of green or another.
Talent – I can speak to the animals and plants of the Enchanted World . . . not to mention the ones in the Faraway Tree.
Favourite Activity – I love to sit peacefully and listen to the constant chatter of all creatures, both big and small.

Favourite Colour – Pink. What other colour would it be? Pink is simply the best colour there is.
Talent – Apart from being a supreme fashion designer, I can also become invisible. It helps me to escape from my screaming fashion fans!
Favourite Activity – Designing. Give me some fabrics and I'll make you something fabulous. Remember – If it's not by Pinx . . . your makeover stinks!

Favourite Colour – Orange. It's the most fun colour of all. It's just bursting with life!
Talent – Being a magician of course. Although I have been known to make the odd Basic Bizzy Blunder with my spells.
Favourite Activity – Baking Brilliant Blueberry Buns and Marvellous Magical Muffins. There is always time to bake a tasty cake to show your friends that you care.

www.blyton.com/enchantedworld

Contents

Introduction

Tucked away among the thickets, groves and forests of our Earth is a special wood. An Enchanted Wood, where the trees grow taller, the branches grow stronger and the leaves grow denser than anywhere else. Search hard enough within this Enchanted Wood, and you'll find one tree that towers above all the others. This is the Faraway Tree, and it is very special. It is home to magical creatures like elves and fairies, even a dragon. But the most magical thing about this very magical Tree? It is the sole doorway to the Lands of the Enchanted World.

Most of the time, the Lands of the Enchanted World simply float along, unattached to anything. But at one time or another, they each come to rest at the top of the Faraway Tree. And if you're lucky enough to be in the Tree at the time, you can climb to its very top, scramble up the long Ladder extending from its tallest branch, push through the clouds and step into that Land.

Of course, there's no telling when a Land will come to the Faraway Tree, or how long it will remain. A Land might stay for months, or be gone within the hour. And if you haven't made it back down the Ladder and into the Faraway Tree before the Land floats away, you could be stuck for a very long time. This is scary even in the most wonderful of Lands, like the Land of Perfect Birthday Parties. But if you get caught in a place like the Land of Ravenous Toothy Beasts, the situation is absolutely terrifying. Yet even though exploring the Lands has its perils, it's also exhilarating, which is why creatures from all over the Enchanted World (and the occasional visiting human) come to live in the Faraway Tree so they can travel from Land to Land.

Of course, not everyone explores the Lands for

pleasure alone. In fact, five fairies have been asked do so for the ultimate cause: to save the life of the Faraway Tree and make sure the doorway to the Enchanted World remains open. These are their stories . . .

Chapter One

Faraway Tree Makeovers

'Voila!' Pinx crowed, standing back to admire her work. 'Tell me that doesn't look magnificent!' Pinx bent down to her customer and added, 'That's just a figure of speech. Don't even dream of actually telling me it doesn't look magnificent.'

The Angry Pixie studied himself in the mirror. His pinched face frowned as he inspected his new look. His goatee beard was dyed purple and plaited with shining strips of light pink fabric; his bald head was covered by a gold-and-red beaded turban, festooned with giant feathers that cascaded over his forehead; his moustache was twisted at the ends and dipped in hot pink wax.

He frowned. He tilted his head first to one

side and then to the other. He fingered the waxy tips of his moustache. Then he raised an eyebrow.

'I like it,' he declared. 'I look . . . fancy.'

He stood up and struck a dignified pose.

'Thank you, Pinx,' he said. 'Thank you very much.'

'My pleasure,' said Pinx. 'And yours, of course.'

As Pinx packed up her supplies and flitted out of the Angry Pixie's home, she called back, 'Remember: "If it's not by Pinx . . ."'

'. . . your makeover stinks!"' finished the Angry Pixie.

Pinx flew home, keeping an eye out for any creatures whose looks she thought she could improve. Life in the Faraway Tree was so much more *fun* now that she had started her new project!

It had all begun a few weeks earlier, soon after Pinx and her friends had successfully returned from the Land of Flora. Ever since Pinx had moved to the Faraway Tree, she had kept herself busy with fun fashion and style challenges, such as redecorating the fairies' treehouse so that everything was upside down. Things like this were fun, but they couldn't compare to the thrill of designing outfits for huge parties like Princess Twilleria's Sweet Centennial or Duchess Eleanorian's Birthday

Ball. Pinx craved something big into which she could sink her teeth.

Finally, inspiration had struck in the form of the most hideous colour clash imaginable. Elf Riverflower – one of the elves who guarded the Vault – darted past Pinx on her way to work, wearing drab olive clothes and carrying a shockingly bright lime wand.

Oh no. Not in Pinx's Tree.

Pinx had pulled Riverflower into her room and refused to let her leave until she was outfitted with twelve spectacular wand-covers, each a perfect match for a fabulous new Pinx-designed outfit, complete with ruffellettas, bubbloons, bells and whistles. Tree residents could hear Riverflower coming from a mile away, and in no time everyone was jealously buzzing about her exciting new look and the amazingly talented fairy behind it. Pinx was in her element again, and it felt phenomenal.

From that moment on, Pinx was inspired. She constantly searched the Faraway Tree for fashion mistakes. As soon as she saw one, she pounced with a cry of, 'Congratulations! You've just earned a Faraway Tree Makeover!' The lucky recipient was always pleased with the result, just like the Angry Pixie; and Pinx was always thrilled to work her makeover magic.

As soon as Pinx soared back into the fairies' large main room, she realised that there would be no more makeovers for a while. The room was as full as it had ever been, most of its space occupied by the hunched-over figure of Gino the Giant. He was nursing a bad cold, and dabbing at his nose with a lacy pink handkerchief, an accessory from his recent Pinx makeover. Silky, Melody, Bizzy and Petal were squashed into the remaining space with Witch Whisper and Cluecatcher. That could only mean one thing . . .

'There's a new Land at the top of the Tree!' Silky called excitedly.

'Great,' said Pinx, trying to echo Silky's enthusiasm.

The truth was that Pinx wasn't sure how she felt about going up into another Land. She was flawless at makeovers, but there were times during the Faraway Fairies' missions that she doubted whether she was doing as much for the team as some of the others.

Melody had transformed herself into Queen Quadrille to outsmart Talon the Troll in the Land of Music. Silky was a brave and quick-thinking leader. Petal had saved her friends by communicating with the flowers in the Land of Flora. Even Bizzy's muddled spells seemed to work out brilliantly in the end. But Pinx . . .

Pinx pushed those thoughts out of her head. She prided herself on being fearless. She could barely admit her worries to herself; she certainly wasn't going to let the others see how she felt.

'So which Land is it?' Pinx asked in the most excited voice she could muster. 'Where are we going next?'

'AAAHHH!' cried Cluecatcher.

All eight of his eyes widened, and his super-sensitive radar dish ears clapped down on his head at the volume of Pinx's exclamation.

'The Land of Giants,' said Witch Whisper,

amused by Pinx's enthusiasm.

'My homeland,' added Gino. 'It's so beautiful. I wish I could go with you, but ... ah ... ah ... ah ... AHHCHOOO!'

His thundering sneeze rocked the room. Witch Whisper waited for the wind to die down and then continued.

'The Land of Giants' Talisman is the Ring of Midnight,' she said. 'It is large enough to fit on the finger of a full-grown giant, with a central stone of the blackest onyx surrounded by diamonds as sparkling as the stars themselves. Not only does it startle everyone with its beauty, but the Ring gives its wearer a sense of absolute power and confidence. If a giant has this prize on his finger, it won't be easy for you to take it back.'

'Especially if it's a Gigante giant,' Gino added.

'What's a Gigante giant?' asked Silky.

'I hope you never have to find out,' Gino

said. 'They're terrible.'

He looked around, as if afraid that a Gigante giant might be within earshot at that very moment. Then he leaned in closer to the fairies.

'There are two kinds of giant in the Land of Giants,' he said, 'There are the Grande giants and the Gigante giants. You can always tell them apart. Grande giants have a mole on their right cheek; Gigante giants have a mole on their left cheek.'

Gino pointed to his own right cheek, on which there was indeed a round mole. He was clearly a Grande giant.

'Never forget the difference,' he warned the fairies.

'What *is* the difference?' Bizzy asked. 'I mean, other than the mole.'

'What's the difference?' Gino squeaked.

It was an odd, frightened sound coming from someone so large. The fairies would have laughed if Gino hadn't looked so serious.

'Grande giants are kind, loving, and generous,' he explained, 'but Gigante giants are bloodthirsty and brutal. They'd rather rip you to shreds than say hello. They're awful! Will you promise me that you will do exactly what the Grande giants do and stay far, far away from any Gigantes?'

'We'll try,' said Petal. 'But what if the Ring is with a Gigante?'

The thought was clearly too terrible for Gino to bear. His eyes widened in shock and then filled with tears. He pulled all five fairies into his arms and hugged them.

'Let's just hope really hard that it's not, OK?' he said with a sob.

After several moments had passed and the fairies were still clutched in Gino's desperate embrace, Witch Whisper cleared her throat.

'We all appreciate your concern, Gino,' she said, 'but it is vital that the fairies make their

way up the Ladder.'

Reluctantly, Gino loosened his grip on the fairies, all of whom were too overwhelmed by Gino's fears even to speak. As they flew out of his arms, he locked eyes with each one of them.

'Be careful,' he said. 'Just promise to me that you will be careful.'

'I'm sure they will, Gino,' said Witch Whisper. 'Thank you for your help.'

She turned to the fairies.

'I believe that you now have all the information you need,' she told them. 'Good luck. We await your successful return.'

The fairies were unusually silent as they flew up to the Ladder at the top of the Tree, stopping along the way to drop off the Eternal Bloom with Zuni and Misty, who would look after her while the fairies were away. (As the only living Talisman to be recovered by the fairies, the Eternal Bloom did not live in the Vault. Instead, she lived with the folk of the Faraway Tree and was guarded at all times by at least one of the residents.)

The fairies could not get Gino's emotional farewell out of their minds. When they finally reached the bottom rung of the Ladder, they paused and looked nervously at each other. Pinx tried to lift their mood.

'Good thing I'm with you lot on this one,' she said. 'If there's one thing I know, it's beautiful jewellery. Of course, there's far more than *one* thing I know . . .'

Her sentence trailed off. After what they had heard from Gino, Pinx was not at all confident that anything she could offer would be truly helpful on this mission. She had been waiting for her chance to shine, but now she was worried that this challenge would be too big.

'When Gino said that the Gigante giants would rather rip us to shreds than say hello, that was just a figure of speech, wasn't it?' said Melody.

The fairies had seen the look on Gino's face when he had said it; none of them believed it was just a figure of speech. Still, they had no desire to admit that out loud.

'Let's just hope the Ladder leads to the Grande giants,' Silky said, 'and that they're the ones who have the Ring.'

Silky looked up towards the top of the Ladder, shrouded by clouds that completely hid whatever dangers awaited them.

'There's only one way to find out,' said Pinx.

She took a deep breath, stepped on to the Ladder and led her friends through the clouds and into the unknown.

Chapter Two

The Land of Giants

The fairies emerged in the middle of a large town. Actually it was a small village by giant standards, filled with tree-lined cobblestone streets and charming cottages. The buildings all had brightly coloured doors, adorned with shiny doorknobs that gleamed in the early evening light. The chimneys on top of the houses happily billowed smoke into the clear blue sky, and the smell of home cooking hung on the breeze.

To the fairies, however, the village was enormous. The cottages loomed above them like skyscrapers and the trees stretched up to the heavens, so high that their tips could not be seen from the ground. The fairies might have floated there for hours, craning their necks at the scale of the scene before them. But then . . .

'AAAHHH!' screamed Melody, leaping away as a razor-sharp claw whooshed past her.

She looked down to see a giant, orange beast – taller than the fairies themselves when it stood on its back paws – crouching on the ground, ready to spring up again.

'Tiger!' Silky cried.

'He's not a tiger,' Petal said breathlessly, as the fairies soared into the air, barely escaping the creature's claws. 'He's just a pussycat.'

'A pussycat?' Pinx exclaimed in disbelief.

'He's a Ferociously Fearsome Feline!' Bizzy added.

'He just wants to play,' Petal told her friends. 'He doesn't realise he's a little big for us.'

The fairies landed in the first safe spot they

saw: a tree branch, high above the cottage roofs. It was the perfect place to catch their breath.

'I like it up here,' Melody said after a moment, as she peered down below. 'Things don't seem quite so . . . giant.'

It was true. From high in the tree, the monster cat didn't look menacing at all. The homes, the streets, the post boxes . . . from their vantage point the fairies could imagine they were all normal-sized and completely harmless.

'You think?' said Pinx. 'Check out this rock.'

The other fairies turned to look at Pinx. She had wandered to the crook of the branch, an area littered with mosses and sticks, and picked up a large white stone. It was so big that she had to cradle it in both her arms.

'It's the size of my pillow,' she declared.

Petal's eyes grew wide.

'Oh Pinx, that's not a rock,' she said, her

voice trembling with fear. 'That's an *egg*. Quick, put it back! If the mother bird thinks we're trying to hurt her baby, she'll –'

'*CAW*!'

They heard a terrible screech and looked up to see an enormous eagle diving towards them. The bird was exactly the same size as the fairies, but with a sharp beak and scythe-like claws that flexed in anticipation of ripping the fairies to shreds.

'FLY!' cried Silky.

The fairies zoomed out of the tree, racing downwards as fast as they could go.

'It's Gaining Ground!' Bizzy wailed. 'Go! Go! Go!'

The fairies sped lower, distancing themselves from the livid eagle.

'MIAOW!' cried the cat, rearing up on its hind legs to swat at the swooping fairies.

Pinx swerved away just in time.

'Look out!' she warned the others.

With the eagle above and the cat below, there was barely room for escape. The fairies could only desperately dart and weave through the streets of the Land of Giants as the vengeful eagle and playful cat gave chase, reaching, swiping, grabbing and continually closing the distance between them.

'There – that way!' Silky screamed, pointing to a large opening in a cottage front door. 'The cat flap!'

The fairies took a sharp right and zipped through the flap, finding themselves in a tremendously large foyer.

'The umbrella stand!' cried Silky.

She pointed at a huge ceramic bowl filled with oversized umbrellas. It was as tall as two fairies, and so heavy that it took all five of them, pushing with all their might, to shove it in front of the cat flap.

WHAM!

The force of the eagle slamming into the

door jolted the fairies away from the umbrella stand and knocked them on to the floor.

'Oh!' Petal cried. 'I hope the mother eagle's OK.'

'You hope the *eagle's* OK?' Pinx exclaimed. 'The eagle wanted to rip us apart!'

'She was only protecting her baby,' retorted Petal, 'which she wouldn't have had to do if *you* hadn't picked up the egg!'

'WHAT'S ALL THAT RACKET?' boomed a deep male voice.

Footsteps echoed through the house. Petal and Pinx forgot their quarrel instantly.

'A giant!' Bizzy whispered.

'A Gigante giant?' asked Melody in a worried voice.

'Hide!' Silky urged, quickly scanning the room. 'There!'

She pointed to a grandfather clock along the wall. It was as tall as seven fairies, and they darted behind it just in time.

'WHAT THE –'

A male giant entered the foyer and stopped in his tracks when he saw the umbrella stand in front of the door. He was enormous, only slightly shorter than the grandfather clock. However, that wasn't what worried the fairies. After all, they were good friends with Gino, who was easily just as large. It was the giant's face that concerned them. He had his back to them, so they couldn't see whether the mole was on his right cheek or his left. What they *could* see was that the giant was wearing a tuxedo.

'I'm sure it was just the kids,' said a second voice.

A female giant clickety-clacked into the hall on high heels, her back to the fairies. She strode to the door and moved the umbrella stand back into its place. As she did so, everyone heard the loud flap of large wings – the eagle was flying back to its nest. Petal breathed a sigh of relief.

The female giant turned to her husband.

'Are you ready?' she asked. 'We have to go. Everyone in town will be there; we don't want to be later than we already are.'

'That dress . . .' Pinx marvelled, leaning out from behind the clock.

She couldn't take her eyes off the female giant's party gown. Even from the back, the flowing lilac taffeta creation was a work of near-perfection. The skirt flounced beautifully at the giant's calves; the thick, jaunty belt around her waist created a stunning silhouette; and the gauzy wrap over her shoulders had a thin piping of . . .

'What is that, satin?' Pinx wondered.

Then she gasped in horror. She had spoken *out loud*!

'What?' said the female giant, turning towards the sound of Pinx's voice.

The other fairies ducked back behind the clock, but Pinx had leaned out too far and didn't have enough time. She froze for a split second, and then squeezed her eyes shut and concentrated on making herself invisible, which was her fairy power. She was just in time.

'What do you mean, "What"?' asked the male giant.

'Didn't you hear something?' asked the female giant.

She looked at the grandfather clock

inquisitively and started to walk towards it, giving Pinx a perfect view of her face . . . and the mole *on her left cheek*. She was a Gigante giant!

Pinx willed herself not to scream, not to gasp, not even to *breathe* as the terrifying giant moved closer. Just as the woman was about to peek behind the clock and discover the other fairies, a wailing cry came from upstairs.

'STOP!' a child's voice shouted, then whined, 'MUM! DAD! BEN'S FEEDING MY BEAR TO THE DOG!'

'*MY* BEAR! *MINE*!' came another screaming voice.

Both giants turned away from the grandfather clock to the staircase behind them.

'Do I have to come up there and sort this out?' the female giant called to her children.

'It's OK,' an older girl's voice replied. 'I've got it under control.'

'Are you sure?' called the mother.

'She's sure,' said her husband. 'Come on, you're right. We have to go.'

He put a comforting hand on his wife's shoulder and called upstairs.

'Kids, we're leaving!' he said. 'Listen to Delania! If you don't, she'll let us know!'

'Yes, Dad,' the children chorused.

The two older giants hurried out through the front door, shutting it behind them. Pinx finally breathed out and became visible again. The other fairies quickly surrounded her, but Silky understood the situation as soon as she saw Pinx's face.

'You saw the mole, didn't you?' she said knowingly.

Pinx nodded.

'Left cheek,' she said. 'Gigantes.'

'And there are more in the house!' Melody cried. 'We have to get out of here!'

'We do,' Pinx agreed, 'before we lose sight

of those giants. We have to follow them to their party.'

'What?' Petal said, gaping at her. 'Have you lost your mind? I know you love parties, but . . .'

She shook her head, completely flummoxed.

'Going to a Gigante Giant Gala sounds like a Grossly Grievous Gaffe,' Bizzy agreed.

'A what?' asked Melody.

'A really, really bad idea,' Bizzy explained.

'Not if we want to find the Ring of Midnight,' Pinx said, her eyes locking with Silky's. 'Those giants were dressed for a very fancy party.'

'The kind of party where you'd wear the best things you have,' Silky agreed.

'Like a ring of onyx surrounded by sparkling diamonds,' added Pinx.

'Pinx is right,' Silky told the others. 'The woman said that everyone in town will be at this party. If the Ring is with the Gigante giants, that's where we'll find it.'

'So,' said Bizzy slowly, hoping that she was mistaken, 'you want us to go to a party filled with Mounds of Massive, Maliciously Malevolent Monsters?'

'Yes,' Pinx said. 'And quickly.'

'OK, kids!' called the older voice from upstairs. 'Let's go down for dinner! Who wants pizza?'

'ME!' roared the children.

Their voices were joined by the deep bark of a giant-sized dog. A stampede of footsteps raced towards the stairs.

'*Now*!' Pinx cried.

The five friends zipped out from behind the clock and out through the cat flap just seconds before the giant children pounded down the stairs. The fairies had a party to attend.

Chapter Three

Melody on Ice

The giant couple hadn't walked far by the time the fairies emerged from the house, so it wasn't difficult to follow them. The fairies kept high above the giants as they flew, and remained on the lookout for any unfriendly birds.

The giants hurried through the cobblestone streets of the town, catching up with several more well-dressed couples, all of whom had the same circular mole on their left cheeks: Gigante giants.

'It's so strange,' Melody whispered, watching the couples walk and chat together. 'They don't seem bloodthirsty at all.'

'Neither did Talon, at first,' Silky remembered. 'They're more dangerous when they hide it.'

'Look at that!' Pinx exclaimed.

The other fairies stared in amazement at the scene below them. The group of giants had come to the end of the road, where a big estate sprawled behind wrought iron gates. The gates stood open, welcoming the giants to an enormous party on a stunningly manicured lawn, which rested at the top of a long, sloping hill. A twelve-piece band played, and dozens of couples twirled on the dance floor, a sea of tuxedos and swirling-skirted gowns. Silk-clothed tables dotted the lawn, and everywhere giants huddled together laughing, chatting, eating and having the time of their lives. But all of them were marked with the same mole on their left cheek that branded them as heartless and evil. It was both magnificent and terrifying at the same time.

'Look at *that*!' Petal added.

The fairies followed her gaze and saw that Silky's crystal necklace was glowing a deep red. Silky smiled.

'The Ring of Midnight is somewhere at this party,' she said. 'Let's find it.'

'How?' asked Melody. 'There are so many of them!'

'We have to stay low,' Silky explained, 'and then they won't see us. Just don't bump into anything.'

'And let's split up,' Petal added. 'If you see anything, call me in your thoughts. I'll hear you, and I can tell everyone else.'

When they had been searching for the Eternal Bloom, the fairies had discovered that, thanks to her fairy power, Petal could hear their thoughts just as clearly as she could hear the thoughts of plants and animals.

'But how do we get in?' Melody asked. 'Staying low is fine, but we're all the way up here. Won't they see us if we suddenly swoop in?'

'Not necessarily,' Pinx said, her face brightening as she had an idea. 'Watch me.'

Before the fairies could say another word, Pinx swooped down and slipped under the long, bubbled skirt of a giant who was just entering the party. A moment later, Petal smiled, and related the words that had just echoed in her head.

'She says, "Are you just going to stand there and gawk, or are you going to join me?"' Petal told them.

'Come on!' Silky said with a grin.

One by one, the fairies swooped down and hid under the skirt of a female giant. They always chose someone at the back of a group so that no other giants would notice, and they picked those with particularly long skirts – ideally with hoops or bubbles. Soon they were all inside the gates.

When they stood on tiptoes, the fairies reached halfway up a giants calf, so staying hidden amid the swirling throng was easy. Staying alive, however, proved to be much more difficult. Hundreds of stilettos, platforms and loafers threatened to skewer and squash them. Tables gave the fairies excellent cover, and were also best for looking for the Ring. The fairies just poked their heads out from under the tablecloths to peer at the fingers of all the giants sitting at the tables.

The plan worked brilliantly . . . for a while. Unfortunately, the closer Melody flew to the band, the harder it was for her to resist the thrum of the brass and the lilt of the woodwind section, and to keep her mind on finding the Ring. When the music soared to a crescendo, Melody couldn't contain herself any longer. She burst out from under her table and twirled gleefully in the air. She remembered to stay low . . . but not low enough to avoid a waiter, who tripped over her and crashed to the floor, sending stuffed

mushrooms skidding across the ground. Several giants gasped and turned to look directly at Melody! Terrified, she thought fast and used her fairy power of transformation to turn herself into an ice statue: a perfect replica of herself.

When the waiter stood up, he noticed the ice sculpture lying on the lawn.

'Well now,' he said aloud. 'How did you get

there? A lovely piece like you should be on the main buffet table.'

Grabbing two cloth napkins to shield his hands from the cold, he lifted ice-Melody in his arms and carried her to a large, round table, which was covered with dishes of sumptuous food and sprays of gorgeous roses. He gave Melody a place of honour at the centre of the table, which was surrounded by Gigante giants loading their plates with food. Melody could not turn back into herself and get away without the giants seeing her!

'Petal?' she thought, willing her friend to hear her. 'I'm on the buffet table, and I think I have a problem. Can you hear me, Petal?'

Suddenly, Melody felt a bead of sweat on her brow. But she couldn't be sweating. She was an ice sculpture! Her gaze fell on the platters of food surrounding her. Each dish was heated by a small burning flame! With so many flames surrounding her, ice-Melody was growing hotter and hotter, and that bead of sweat she felt rolling down her brow was the first sign of melting!

Melody tried to concentrate on maintaining her shape, but it was no use. The hot dishes and naked flames were becoming too much for her. She had to do something.

'Petal!' Melody cried in her thoughts. 'Help me! I can't get away . . . and I'm *melting*!'

At the other side of the party, Petal heard Melody's cry and relayed the message to all the other fairies. Pinx, Petal, Silky and Bizzy peered out from underneath their tables and gasped.

'Don't worry, Melody!' Petal silently assured her friend, 'We'll do something – I promise!'

Petal exchanged panicked glances with Silky, Pinx and Bizzy. They could see beads of water gathering all over Melody, but she was completely surrounded by Gigante giants enjoying their buffet. What could the fairies possibly do to help her?

Chapter Four

Pinx Gets the Ring

Petal was about to ask the rose sprays on the buffet table to fling themselves into the giants' faces to create a distraction, so that Melody could transform, when a particularly important-looking giant stood up at the head table, tapping his glass with a fork to get everyone's attention.

While all the giants at the party were well dressed, this one had a special air of elegance. He was carrying a cane and wearing a top hat and a black, velvet cloak, lined in plush red. However, the only thing that Melody noticed was the ring on his right hand: a thick platinum band encircling a massive, square-cut stone of the blackest onyx, surrounded by diamonds as sparkling as the stars themselves.

Its beauty was exquisite, as was the sense of power it gave off. You didn't have to know the Ring of Midnight was a Talisman to appreciate its strength. Witch Whisper was right; it would not be easy to convince this giant to give it up.

The giant's important position was made even more evident by the reaction he received from the other guests. When he tapped his glass, the band stopped playing, the dancers stood still and all conversation and movement ended. Every giant turned to listen, including the giants around the buffet table. With all eyes on the giant with the Ring, it was safe for Melody to turn back into herself and dart under Petal's table, where the other fairies joined them, enveloping Melody in a huge hug.

'That giant has the Ring of Midnight!' Melody told them.

At the front of the room, the band leader

tapped on the microphone.

'Ladies and gentleman,' he said. 'I present Lord Aurelio.'

Lord Aurelio smiled graciously as he took the microphone.

'Thank you, everyone, for coming to this party to honour my only child, my daughter, Julia.'

He gestured to a lovely young giant at the head table, who smiled as everyone applauded.

'As you know,' Lord Aurelio continued, 'my daughter has reached the age at which she will wed, and it is my pleasure to announce her engagement to Parrino.'

Lord Aurelio now gestured to the handsome giant sitting next to Julia, who beamed as the crowd applauded him. Parrino took Julia's hand and looked at her lovingly. Julia gave him a weak smile in return and then looked down at her lap.

'She doesn't want to marry him,' Pinx realised.

'What? Who?' asked Silky.

She had been concentrating only on Lord Aurelio's Ring, and barely paying attention to what he was saying.

'Julia,' Pinx elaborated. 'She doesn't want to marry Parrino. I've been to a lot of engagement parties, and that's not how happy brides-to-be behave.'

'And now,' Lord Aurelio continued, 'let us

celebrate with Julia and Parrino as they share their first dance as future husband and wife.'

Lord Aurelio led the crowd in applause and then strode back to his place at the head table as the band struck up a song. Parrino took Julia's hand and led her to the dance floor.

'Everyone's watching the couple,' Silky noted. 'Let's head to Lord Aurelio's table and see if we can get the Ring.'

Darting between tables, ducking under tablecloths and serving carts, and always staying below the giants' line of sight, the fairies flitted their way to the head table. Lord Aurelio was sitting in the centre, his hands in his lap. The Ring of Midnight was so close that the fairies could touch it, and Silky's crystal necklace glowed its deepest red.

'OK,' said Silky, 'if we all grab it, we can slide it off really gently. If he's paying close enough attention to the dancing, he won't even notice.'

'You just want to *take* it?' Melody asked, aghast.

'What else should we do?' Pinx retorted. '*Ask* him for it? He's a Gigante giant. What do you think he'll say?'

Melody looked uncomfortable.

'I don't like it,' she said.

'I don't either,' Bizzy agreed. 'It feels like stealing.'

'*Technically* it isn't,' Petal said. 'I mean, the Ring isn't *really* Lord Aurelio's.'

'Petal!' Melody gasped in surprise.

'What?' Petal replied, 'I don't like it either, but you know what Gino told us about Gigante giants. I don't want to upset them.'

'We have no choice,' Silky agreed. 'We need to take the Talisman and get as far away from the Gigante giants as possible.'

Bizzy and Melody reluctantly agreed. Much as they hated the idea of taking the Talisman, they hated the idea of failing their mission even more.

On Silky's cue, each of the fairies grabbed a section of the ring and pulled. Compared to the fairies it was the size of a large birthday cake. However, it was heavy with gems and precious metals, and the fairies had to use all their strength in order to slip it down Lord Aurelio's finger unnoticed. Just a little bit further . . . a little bit further . . .

'Super-Sweet Success!' Bizzy cried excitedly as the Ring slipped all the way off Lord Aurelio's finger and into the fairies' arms.

Unfortunately, Bizzy also threw her arms into the air in celebration, and when she let go of the heavy Ring, the other fairies were thrown off-balance and lost their grip. The Ring clanked loudly against the legs of Lord Aurelio's chair as it clattered to the ground. Lord Aurelio immediately pushed back his chair and peered under the table, while the fairies flew as high as they could, pressing their backs against the underside of the table so they wouldn't be seen.

'My ring!' cried Lord Aurelio.

He reached for it, but the Ring seemed to struggle to push itself up on to its side. Lord Aurelio was so astounded that he could only watch, flabbergasted, as the Ring fully righted itself and then began to roll away.

'Pinx,' Silky whispered in excitement.

Realising that their best chance of taking the Ring was about to disappear, Pinx had made herself invisible and hoisted the Ring on to its side. With the Ring upright, Pinx could fly very low to the ground and roll it along in front of her.

Lord Aurelio broke out of his stunned stare and tried to stand upright . . . smashing his head on the underside of the table.

'OW!' he cried.

He staggered out from under the table and hoisted himself to his full height.

'MY RING!' he bellowed. 'IT'S ROLLING AWAY!'

As always when Lord Aurelio spoke, all the other giants paid attention.

'I'll get it, Daddy!' Julia cried, breaking away from Parrino to chase after the Ring. 'Everyone, let me through!'

She tore through the crowd after the Ring, but Pinx had quite a head start, and had already reached the edge of the party area, where the lawn gave way to a rolling hill that

led down to a thick grove of trees. The Ring zoomed downhill and Pinx grinned as she flew after it. Finally, the Ring zipped into the grove of trees, bouncing over the roots and undergrowth until it fell on its side and stopped.

Pinx thought that she had escaped . . . until the thundering footsteps of Julia the giant made the ground beneath her shake. Pinx stayed invisible and tried to cover the Ring with a pile of fallen leaves, but she wasn't fast enough.

‘There you are,’ Julia said, reaching down to pick up the Ring.

‘No way,’ Pinx said to herself. ‘We worked too hard for this.’

With all her might, Pinx gripped the Ring. She dug her feet into the earth and pulled, determined to keep it away from the giant.

Julia was shocked to find the Ring so much heavier than she had expected. She let go in surprise, and sent Pinx staggering backwards, the Ring smacking hard into her stomach.

‘OOF!’ grunted Pinx.

The shock of the tumble made her lose concentration and she instantly became visible again.

Melody, Petal, Silky and Bizzy had managed to get away from the party without being seen and had flown straight down to the grove. They had hoped to celebrate their success and fly immediately to the Ladder, but their eyes widened in horror when they saw

Julia the Gigante giant pick up their friend.

A smile spread across the giant's face as she looked down at the dazed fairy.

'Hello,' she said. 'What are you?'

Chapter Five

Pinx's Plan

As Pinx's friends looked on breathlessly, Julia raised a thick finger and brushed it gently against Pinx's face.

'Hey,' the giant cooed softly. 'Are you OK?'

Silky, Melody, Petal and Bizzy looked at each other in surprise. Was this the terrible temper of the bloodthirsty Gigante giants?

'She's pretending to be nice,' Silky whispered. 'We just need to wait for the right moment, then we'll get Pinx away from her.'

'This must be awfully heavy for you,' Julia said, lifting the Ring out of Pinx's arms and placing it in her pocket. 'There . . . now you can breathe.'

Cradled in Julia's palm, the weight of the Ring off her chest, Pinx blinked and realised

that she was face to face with a left-cheek-moled Gigante giant. She started to struggle.

'Let go of me!' she roared.

'OK,' Julia said, spreading out her hand so that Pinx could fly off. 'Is that better?'

Pinx frowned in bewilderment. Wasn't it supposed to be a little more difficult than that to escape a Gigante giant?

'Yes . . . thank you,' Pinx replied.

'I'm Julia,' said the giant.

She moved her arm swiftly and Pinx darted away to avoid the expected blow, but Julia was only holding out her free hand for Pinx to shake.

'I'm Pinx,' Pinx replied, taking two of Julia's fingers in her hand and shaking them warily.

'You're a fairy, aren't you?' Julia said with a grin. 'You look just like the pictures of wish-granting fairies from my storybooks, except much more beautiful, of course. And I love those leggings. Do you think they'd look good on someone as tall as me, or would the pattern be too much?'

'They'd look fabulous on you!' Pinx gasped. 'Especially if I made them. For someone your height I'd use this shimmery satinella –'

Pinx stopped herself and stared at Julia, who had sat down on a tree stump and was gazing avidly at Pinx as she listened to the fashion advice.

'I'm sorry, but I have to ask,' Pinx said. 'Before I start imagining your perfect makeover . . . are we anywhere near the part where you rip me to shreds?'

'Rip you to . . .' Julia stammered. 'What are you talking about?'

'Well, you *are* a Gigante giant, aren't you?' Pinx asked. 'I mean, I can see the mole on your left cheek, so . . .'

Julia rolled her eyes.

'You must have been talking to a Grande giant,' she said.

'The Grande giants are wrong?' Melody asked.

Pinx and Julia turned at the sound of her voice.

'My friends!' cried Pinx.

The five fairies flew together for a huge hug, after which Pinx introduced them all to Julia. Julia offered them each her hand, and they shook her fingers . . . all except Silky. She folded her arms and frowned at Julia.

'One of our close friends is a Grande giant,' Silky declared. 'He warned us that the Gigante giants are bloodthirsty savages. Are you suggesting that he lied to us?'

'"Bloodthirsty savages"?' repeated Julia. 'Oh well, I suppose that's just as bad as what most Gigantes would say about the Grandes. It's crazy. The groups have been feuding forever; I don't think anyone even remembers why. I know I don't.'

Julia took a deep breath and then leaned forwards to look Silky in the eye.

'Your friend wasn't lying to you,' she said. 'I'm sure he thought he was telling the absolute truth. He just doesn't know any better.'

'So, if you're not a Voraciously Vicious Villain,' Bizzy said, 'maybe you can help us!'

'Help you with what?' asked Julia.

The fairies told her all about their mission,

the Talismans, the Faraway Tree, Talon and why the fate of the entire Enchanted World depended on them returning the Ring of Midnight to the Vault. Julia hung on every word, and when they were finished she immediately leaped up from the tree stump.

'I'd love to help you!' she said.

'Great!' Pinx cried. 'Give us the Ring and we'll take it to the Ladder right now!'

'I can't,' said Julia with a sigh. 'Not now. My dad's crazy about that Ring. I told him I'd bring it back, and if I don't, he'll be so angry . . . believe me, he's not a fun person when he's that cross.'

'Isn't there any way you can convince him?' pleaded Silky.

'To give up his Ring?' Julia laughed. 'His most prized possession? Never. There's only one way he'll hand over this Ring: he'll give it to me on my wedding day.'

Suddenly her face fell, and she sat back

down on the tree stump.

'And that's not far away,' she added in a low voice.

Silky looked at Julia with sympathy.

'You don't want to marry Parrino, do you?' she asked.

Julia shook her head.

'He's very nice, but I don't love him,' she said. 'Can you imagine marrying someone you don't love?'

The fairies shook their heads; none of them could.

'You should tell your father the truth,' Petal said. 'He loves you; he'll understand.'

'Of course he will,' Julia agreed. 'He'll tell me that he'd be delighted to see me marry a man I love – who's the lucky guy? And then I'll tell him it's Romero, a Grande giant, and he'll lock me in my room for the rest of my life. I don't even want to think what he'd do to Romero.'

'You're in love with a Grande giant?' Pinx said with a gasp.

Julia nodded miserably.

'We met in the woods between our two realms,' she said. 'It was love at first sight, but neither of us could tell anyone. We try to see each other as often as we can, but it always has to be in secret.'

'That's so romantic!' Melody sighed.

'It's like a Marisolode movie!' Bizzy added.

'It's torture, that's what it is!' wailed Julia. 'And now that it's my marrying year, my father won't rest until I'm married to a nice Gigante giant. I'll be Mrs Parrino and I'll never see my Romero again.'

Her voice faltered and grew soft.

'I can't bear it,' she said. 'I don't know what to do, but I can't bear it.'

Julia started to cry, and Pinx placed a hand on her shoulder.

'Wait,' Pinx said. 'What if you were to

marry Romero . . . would Lord Aurelio still give you the Ring?'

'He would only give me the Ring if he approved of the wedding,' said Julia, 'which he would never, *never* –'

'What if we found a way of *making* him approve?' Pinx interrupted. 'Would he give you the Ring then?'

'Well, yes, but . . .' Julia stammered.

'And if he *did* give you the Ring,' Pinx continued, 'would you give it to us? To thank us for bringing you and Romero together?'

'If you could do that, I'd give you the Enchanted World!' Julia cried. 'The universe! I'd give you *anything*!'

'The Ring is all we need,' smiled Pinx. 'Do we have a deal?'

Julia's eyes grew wide as she realised that Pinx was serious.

'Yes!' she shouted, leaping up in delight. 'Yes! Yes! A million times yes! What do we do first? Wait – I have to return Daddy's Ring first. I'll come right back! Promise you won't go anywhere? Oh, this is the best day of my life! Wait until I tell Romero – the storybooks were right – fairies *do* grant wishes!'

Julia danced off, half-twirling, half-running as she raced back to the party to return the Ring to her father. Pinx watched her happily . . . until she was nearly bowled over by Bizzy wrapping her in an elated embrace.

'I love it!' Bizzy cried. 'The Strategy's Simply Sensational! We get the Ring *and* save true love!'

'It's a great plan, Pinx,' Silky added. 'How do we do it?'

Pinx looked around and realised that all her friends were looking at her with open faces, eagerly awaiting her thoughts.

'You want *me* to come up with the plan?' she asked.

'Of course,' Silky replied. 'It's your idea. You'll know how to do it better than anyone.'

Pinx felt a glow of pleasure at Silky's confidence in her. She took a deep breath and tried to hide her unease.

'You're right,' Pinx replied, 'and I'll tell you exactly what my plan is . . . as soon as I've come up with one.'

Chapter Six

Romero's Balcony

It took Julia no time at all to deliver the Ring to her father and race back to the fairies. She couldn't bear to be at the engagement party a second longer – not when she could be planning her future with Romero! She had claimed that she was feeling sick in order to get out of the party. It wasn't really a lie; she *was* sick – heartsick at the idea of marrying Parrino instead of Romero.

'So, what's our first step?' Julia asked Pinx in excitement.

The other fairies looked at Pinx expectantly – what *was* their first step?

'The first thing we need to know,' said Pinx, 'is whether Romero loves you as much as you love him.'

'He does!' Julia exclaimed. 'At least . . . I think he does. I mean, he *says* he does. I don't know . . . how can I know?'

'*We'll* know,' Pinx assured her. 'What do you think, Bizzy? Seen enough Marisolode movies to know true love when you see it?'

'I've seen them all!' Bizzy enthused. '*Love's Lost Labours, The Many Loves of Windsor, All's Well That Loves Well* –'

'See?' Pinx said to Julia, 'We'll recognise true love. Now tell me, how do you and Romero arrange to meet?'

'We can't,' said Julia. 'We go to the woods a lot and hope to run into one another. A couple of times he has surprised me by showing up at my window at night and serenading me.'

'I love that!' squealed Melody. 'Have you ever done that for him?'

'Sung to him at his window?' Julia asked. 'Isn't that just a boy thing?'

'Not necessarily,' said Petal.

'Not at *all*!' added Silky.

'Romance is for everyone,' Bizzy sighed happily.

'Exactly,' said Pinx in a firm tone. 'There is nothing wrong with a girl showing a boy how she feels. Can you get us to Romero's house?'

'Of course!' said Julia. 'I mean, we'd have to be very careful, because it's in Grande territory, but . . . do you really think I can do it?'

'Not dressed like that you can't,' Pinx declared. 'First stop, your room. I need to see everything in your wardrobe and make-up kit. You're about to have a Faraway Tree Makeover!'

Two hours later, Julia and the fairies were tiptoeing across Romero's family estate, deep in Grande giant territory. Julia had been transformed. She was wearing patterned leggings just like Pinx, but in a shimmery satinella that perfectly complemented her exceptionally long body. Over the leggings, Pinx had created a flowing blue tunic, with a gauzy poofled skirt and fuzzy-furrino shoulder wrap in a lighter shade of blue. Pinx had piled Julia's hair on top of her head, and shining tendrils hung down to frame her face, which Pinx had dusted with glitter to make her features sparkle.

'I feel like a princess,' Julia breathed excitedly, catching sight of her reflection in a darkened window.

'Now all you need is a prince,' Pinx declared.

'That's his room,' Julia said, pointing to a balcony directly above her, at the end of a rose-vine covered trellis.

'That means that you should stand *here*,' Petal said, looking around at the neat but ordinary lawn around them. 'Not the most romantic spot . . . yet.'

Petal flew to the trellis and whispered to its

flowers, which seemed to bloom larger as they listened. Eager to help, the rose vines crawled down from the wall and along the ground to Julia. The vines leaped over the giant in graceful arcs, framing her in a half-dome of stunning blooms.

'Are you ready?' Melody asked Julia.

Julia nodded, although she looked rather nervous.

'All it takes is a magical rap at the window to get his attention,' said Bizzy.

She raised her arms, stared up at the balcony and cried, 'Ratata-tara-paloodle-loo!'

Instantly, a huge, hungry *rat* appeared on Romero's balcony, as large as the fairies themselves. Before the fairies and Julia could react, the ravenous rat scuttled into the room, through the door, which stood ajar.

'AAARGH!' came a cry from Romero's room.

Seconds later, a handsome young giant staggered out on to the balcony, wrestling the massive, toothy rodent away from his throat.

'Oops,' Bizzy winced. 'Basic Bizzy Blunder!'

She quickly called out a counterspell and the rat disappeared.

'Now!' hissed Pinx.

Before the confused Romero could get his bearings, Silky flew high above and used her fairy power of illumination to shine a spotlight on to Julia, who was framed perfectly in the half-dome of roses. Melody began to hum a beautiful tune, nodding at Julia in encouragement. Julia took a deep breath and began to sing the song that Melody had taught her while she was having her makeover.

'My bounty is as boundless as the sea, my love as deep; the more I give to thee, the more I have, for both are infinite.'

Julia's lovely voice caressed each word of

the song as she gazed into Romero's eyes.

'Look at him,' Bizzy whispered to the other Fairies. 'He loves her!'

Bizzy was right. Although he was still tousled and rumpled from sleep and his rat encounter, Romero was gazing down at Julia in pure rapture, his face aglow with adoration. Without taking his eyes off her for a second, Romero vaulted over his balcony and climbed down the trellis. He walked slowly towards her and, without saying a word, he held out his arm. Julia smiled and accepted his unspoken offer, taking his hand. As Melody continued to hum their song, the two giants danced together in the glow of Silky's light.

The fairies were absolutely entranced by Julia and Romero's beautiful dance, which is why none of them realised that they were in danger until it was too late.

'NOW!' boomed a voice.

A stream of armed giants poured out of a

lower room in the mansion. Several of them threw a net over the fairies while the rest grabbed Julia and Romero, pulling them apart.

'Wait!' cried Romero, struggling against his captors. 'What are you doing?'

A massive giant swept out of the house, wrapped in a robe of sumptuous velvet. Everything about the man exuded strength and power, and when he spoke, the fairies recognised the booming voice that had given the order. They stopped wrestling against the net and listened.

'I heard your scream, Romero,' the giant said. 'You can imagine my horror when I looked outside and saw this *Gigante* giant trying to bewitch you into her clutches. Naturally, I called the guards immediately.'

'Father, no!' cried Romero. 'You don't understand! I'm not bewitched!'

Romero's father was not listening. He

strode towards Julia, who was straining against the tight hold of the guards. Romero's father gave a grim smile.

'Julia . . .' he said. 'Lord Aurelio's daughter. So he thought you could kidnap my boy using magic? I'd like to see your father's face when he hears that *you've* been captured.'

'Lord Domino, please listen –' Julia began.

'Take her away!' Lord Domino told his guards. 'And her wicked sprites as well!'

'"Wicked sprites"?' Pinx exclaimed.

She tried to zoom forwards to give Lord Domino a piece of her mind, but she just got tangled in the net.

'Blast this thing open, Silky!' she cried. 'No one talks to us like that!'

'Not yet,' said Silky, shaking her head. 'We need to stay with Julia to make sure that she's OK.'

The other fairies knew that she was right, but as the guards roughly dragged them along behind Julia, they were all tortured by the same thoughts. If they didn't escape now, would they have the chance later? And even if they did, how in the world would they get the Gigante and Grande giants to agree to a wedding between Julia and Romero, so that the fairies could get the Ring of Midnight?

The Great Escape?

The Grande giant guards dragged Julia and the fairies deep into a dark, underground prison. As soon as the guards left, Silky lit the room with a gentle glow. The fairies were crammed into a small wire cage. It was tucked in the corner of a larger cage in which Julia was crouching.

'So much for the perfect romantic evening,' she said.

Her voice was hollow with fear and despair. The fairies exchanged worried glances.

'If it makes you feel any better,' Petal said, 'Romero really does love you. We could tell.'

'What does it matter?' Julia cried. 'His kind will never accept me, and my kind will never accept him!'

‘There has to be a way to change their minds,’ Melody insisted.

Silky shook her head.

‘It could take a lifetime,’ she said, ‘and where does that leave Julia and Romero?’

‘If only you and Romero lived in the Faraway Tree, like Gino,’ Bizzy sighed, looking at Julia. ‘Then nothing could stop your Lifelong Lasting Love.’

‘That’s it!’ Pinx shouted, staring at Julia in excitement. ‘You and Romero can come and live in the Faraway Tree! You can get married and be happy there. It makes perfect sense!’

‘But if Julia and Romero come to live in the Faraway Tree, they might never see their families again,’ Petal pointed out.

‘Maybe not,’ Julia said, looking thoughtful, ‘but if we stay here I’ll have to marry Parrino and give up Romero forever.’

She stood up, her eyes shining with a new determination.

'Let's do it,' she said. 'I want to live in the Faraway Tree. Romero will too – I know it.'

'Fantastic!' Pinx exclaimed. 'OK, the first thing we have to do is to get out of these cages. Then we –'

'Wait!' Silky interrupted. 'What about the Ring of Midnight? If we're not getting Lord Aurelio's blessing for the wedding, we won't get the Ring.'

'*I'll* get the Ring,' Julia said. 'My father puts it in a safe when he goes to bed; I know the combination.'

'But you said that you couldn't take the Ring,' Melody objected. 'You said that your father would get so angry –'

'That was when I thought I'd be staying in the Land of Giants,' Julia replied. 'If I'm not here, he can get as angry as he wants. Besides, it's for a good cause, right?'

'The future of the entire Enchanted World,' Bizzy said, nodding.

'So it's settled,' said Julia. 'We'll get out of here, grab the Ring, get Romero and escape to the Faraway Tree.'

Julia's eyes flashed with excitement at the adventure of it all, and the fairies couldn't help but get caught up in her enthusiasm.

'OK then,' Silky grinned. 'Everyone stand back.'

The fairies crowded behind Silky and Julia edged to a far corner of her cage. Silky screwed up her eyes and concentrated, and a ray of light shot out from her body, burning through the wire of the fairies' cage. They all flitted out through the gaping hole.

'One down, one to go,' Silky said.

She concentrated again, shooting a powerful beam of light into the bars of the larger cage.

Nothing happened.

Silky tried harder, focusing all her energy into a super-concentrated beam of light.

The bars smouldered, but they didn't break.

'I can't,' Silky gasped, panting from the effort. 'The bars are too thick. If I try any harder . . .'

'You don't need to,' Melody said, putting a comforting hand on Silky's shoulder. 'We can find another way.'

'Like unlocking the door!' Bizzy suggested, flying up to the large padlock that secured Julia's cage. 'All we need is a key.'

Bizzy closed her eyes, waved her arms, and

cried, 'Skeebledee-freebledee-keebledee-skree!' As she finished her spell, she thrust her arms out at the padlock on the cage door.

The padlock shivered as Bizzy's magic hit it, and the shiver travelled from the lock to the cage bars and down to the ground, from which a deep, rumbling roar began to sound.

'Uh-oh,' Bizzy said, cringing.

Julia and the fairies backed as far away from the roaring spot of ground as possible. The earth itself seemed to churn and roll, and then the result of Bizzy's spell burst up from the ground.

'A *tree*!' cried Petal delightedly.

A massive, fully grown oak tree had emerged from the ground beneath their prison. Its trunk was so strong and thick that it lifted one side of the cage as it grew, tilting it higher and higher . . .

'You're brilliant, Bizzy!' Silky shouted as the bars of the cage bent enough for Julia to

crawl through. 'Let's go!'

As the colossal tree trunk continued to grow, Julia and the fairies ran past it and raced up the stairs of the underground prison. There were no guards, but when they burst out through the door into the night, a shrill alarm sounded to warn the Grandes of their escape.

'The woods!' Silky cried.

Julia and the fairies raced for the dense woods ahead of them, zooming over boulders and through brambles for what seemed like hours, until the sound of the alarm was far behind them and they knew they weren't being followed. When they finally had a moment to catch their breath, Julia looked around.

'I recognise this,' she said.

Thanks to her secret meetings with Romero, she knew the woods between Grande and Gigante territory very well.

'We're not far from my father's house,' Julia told the fairies. 'We'll have the Ring soon.'

The fairies followed Julia through the woods, but just as they finally emerged into Gigante territory, they heard another booming voice.

'HALT!'

The angry shout stopped them in their tracks. Immediately, a horde of soldiers bearing drawn swords darted out from the cover of the trees and surrounded the fairies.

The super-sharp tips of their bristling swords were pointing directly at the fairies, almost touching their chests.

Chapter Eight

Pinx – Party Planner Extraordinaire

As the fairies cringed back from the sword tips, Parrino strode into the circle of soldiers. Anger raged in his eyes, and he glared furiously at the five friends.

'Who are you and what are you doing with my fiancée?' he growled. 'Speak quickly – your lives depend on the answer!'

'Parrino, no!' cried Julia. 'These fairies are my friends!'

Parrino looked confused.

'Your friends?' he asked.

'Her *friends*,' Pinx told him. 'Which means the swords go away, right?'

Pinx tried to push a sword away from her, and then pulled her hand back from the sharp edge. The soldiers remained motionless, awaiting orders from Parrino.

'This doesn't make sense,' Parrino said. 'Your father got a message from the Grandes to say that you had been taken prisoner. I gathered troops to come and rescue you.'

'It was the *fairies* who rescued me, Parrino,' Julia retorted. 'So can you call off the soldiers?'

Parrino glared at the fairies suspiciously.

'Not yet,' he said. 'We've never had fairies in the Land of Giants. How do I know we can trust them? They might have bewitched you.'

'You could believe our word of honour,' suggested Melody.

'They saved me, Parrino.' Julia insisted. 'You can trust them.'

'Convince me,' Parrino demanded. 'Tell me everything. How did the Grandes take you? Who was responsible? How did these fairies know you needed help?'

Julia opened her mouth to speak . . . and then shut it again almost immediately. The fairies looked at one another, aware of what she was thinking. How could Julia explain things to Parrino without risking Romero's safety by admitting her feelings for him?

'No explanation?' asked Parrino. 'Then I have one of my own. I think your 'rescuers' are Grande spies, and I should dispose of them right now!'

'Wait!' screeched Pinx, turning to Julia. 'Julia, I think it's time to tell Parrino the whole truth.'

Julia's eyes widened in alarm.

'The whole truth?' she repeated.

'About your true feelings,' Pinx went on.

Silky, Bizzy, Melody and Petal stared at her – what was Pinx doing?!

'I . . . I can't.' stammered Julia.

'Of course you can, you silly thing!' said Pinx.

She closed her eyes and made herself invisible. The soldiers gasped as she reappeared next to Parrino.

'You're a very lucky man,' Pinx said. 'This woman is absolutely crazy about you.'

'She is?' asked Parrino.

'She is?' echoed Bizzy.

Silky elbowed her in the ribs.

'She is,' Pinx confirmed. 'She would *have* to be to plan such a crazy hoax just to surprise you with the most amazing wedding ever.'

'I don't understand . . .' Parrino said, looking completely confused.

'The message about Julia being taken prisoner wasn't sent by the Grandes,' said Pinx. 'It was sent by *Julia*, so you wouldn't suspect that she was actually meeting the most fabulous party organiser in the entire Enchanted World – me!'

'You're a . . . party organiser?' Parrino asked.

'The *best* party organiser,' Pinx emphasised. 'Didn't you hear about Duchess Eleanorian's Birthday Ball? Princess Twilleria's Sweet Centennial?'

'No, I didn't,' Parrino said with deep suspicion.

Pinx's jaw dropped.

'I don't appreciate your tone, sir,' she said. 'Are you *doubting* me?'

Pinx turned to Julia.

'I'm sorry, Julia,' she said. 'I know how long you tried to get an appointment with me, and I know how badly you wanted to make everything perfect for this fiancé of yours, but if he's such an idiot that he can't appreciate the kind of event I'm offering . . .'

Pinx turned to fly away.

'Wait!' Parrino cried.

Pinx turned slowly back to face him, her arms folded.

'I didn't mean to insult you,' Parrino apologised. 'It's just . . . why go to all the trouble of faking a message from the Grandes? Couldn't Julia just have met you secretly in the woods? And how could she have been trying to get an appointment with you for weeks when our engagement was only announced tonight?'

Pinx was stumped, but Silky jumped in.

'Just because you weren't officially engaged, that doesn't mean Julia wasn't secretly hoping and planning for it,' she said.

'Exactly,' Pinx confirmed with relief.

'And the Crazy Cover-up was because she's a Blushing Bride-to-Be!' Bizzy added. 'They can Be Beyond Batty . . . Basically Blithering!'

Parrino turned to Julia, looking for confirmation. Julia gave a nervous smile.

'Blithering!' she repeated.

'I . . . I don't know what to say,' Parrino stammered.

'How about, "Put down the swords"?' Pinx suggested. 'I'm not used to having my staff held at swordpoint and I don't like it at all.'

'Forgive me,' Parrino said.

He signalled for the soldiers to lower the swords surrounding Melody, Petal, Silky and Bizzy.

'So, now I'll continue with what I was about to tell Julia before we were so rudely interrupted,' Pinx said with a baleful glare at Parrino, who lowered his head. 'I *can* organise your wedding, but I'm very booked up, so it has to be tomorrow.'

'Tomorrow?' Julia gasped, horrified.

'*Tomorrow*,' Pinx repeated. 'And I won't do it for just half the Land. I want *everyone* to see my work. That means that every giant in the Land is invited, Gigante *and* Grande.'

'But that's insane!' Parrino argued. 'The Grande giants are evil, hideous creatures! I'd rather invite a pit of venomous snakes to my wedding!'

'That's up to you,' Pinx said with a shrug. 'Sorry it couldn't work out, Julia.'

Pinx gave Julia a meaningful look, and Julia grabbed Parrino's hand and looked up at him lovingly.

'Oh please, darling!' Julia cried. 'I know it's crazy, but it's the only way Pinx will do the wedding! And a Pinx wedding . . . it's what I've dreamed of.'

Parrino looked down at Julia's lovely face and his expression softened.

'All right,' he said, 'if that's what you really want. We'll spread the word to the Grandes . . . but we'll have the event well guarded. If one of them makes a false move . . .'

'You'll crush them,' Julia finished for him.

'I'm sorry I spoiled your surprise,' Parrino said. 'I'll leave you and the fairies to your planning. After all, it's bad luck to see the bride before the wedding.'

He kissed Julia on the cheek and walked away with his soldiers. Julia kept a fixed smile on her face until he was out of sight, and then turned on Pinx.

'I'm marrying *Parrino* tomorrow night?' she said through gritted teeth. 'I hope you have some kind of plan?'

'Of course I have a plan,' Pinx grinned. 'My plan is to put together the most astounding wedding that the Enchanted World has ever seen.'

Chapter Nine

A Giant Wedding

The next twenty-four hours were the busiest in Pinx's life. She never made promises lightly, but this time she had more at stake than ever before. Pinx knew that she had pinned their hopes of regaining the Ring of Midnight on one night and also that her meddling could alter the future of two lovers. She couldn't let them down. This was her big chance to help the team, and of course it never hurt to carry out a few makeovers in the process. If she was going to organise the most stupendous wedding the Enchanted World had ever seen, she had massive amounts of work to do, and sleep was not an option.

First, there was the question of location. The ceremony had to be somewhere huge enough to hold everyone in the Land of Giants, but neutral enough that neither the Grande nor Gigante giants would feel uncomfortable. After flying all over the Land with Silky, Petal, Melody and Bizzy, Pinx found the perfect spot: a massive clearing within the woods that separated the two territories.

Of course, making such an enormous space look truly spectacular was a task worthy of weeks of Pinx's time. Unfortunately, she didn't have that luxury. She quickly had Bizzy magic up enough giant-sized seating to accommodate everyone. (Well, it didn't really happen *quickly*, as first Bizzy magicked up an assortment of *meats* instead of seats. And while the meats would come in very handy for the reception after the ceremony, they of course had to be gathered and cooked and refrigerated. So the whole thing actually took quite a while, but Bizzy did eventually get around to magicking up enough gorgeously gilded giant-sized seats for all the guests.)

As soon as the seats were in place, Pinx put Silky and Petal on decorations duty, giving them a detailed list of instructions. Petal was in charge of convincing the most stunning flowers in the Land to uproot themselves and move to the wedding area. Silky was in charge of fabric bunting, which had to be found; dyed fuchsia, turquoise and white (Pinx's choice for the wedding colours); and strung expertly from every tree and chair until the clearing became a colourful wonderland.

The music for the wedding had to be spectacular, so Pinx put Melody on the task. Melody knew exactly what she wanted to play as the guests entered, and Pinx loved it. But when it came to the song Melody would sing as Julia walked down the aisle, Pinx shook her head critically at Melody's every suggestion. One was too bouncy, another was

too simple, another too ordinary . . . none of them was right. Finally Melody threw up her hands and started singing the one song she knew was totally wrong, and Pinx's eyes lit up.

'Yes!' Pinx cried. 'That's the one!'

'Really?' Melody asked in surprise.

'It's absolutely perfect,' Pinx insisted. 'Find the best Gigante musicians and make sure they know it in time for Julia to walk down the aisle.'

Then there was the matter of the invitations. Obviously, it was too late to send personalised notes to every single giant in the Land. The answer? Skywriting. Pinx worked with Bizzy to help her magic up a concoction of fuchsia, turquoise and white smoke that would stream from Bizzy's feet as she flew. Then Bizzy went soaring across the Land, zipping acrobatically through the air to scrawl the wedding invitation in the sky from horizon to horizon and make sure no giant missed it.

By the time all this was settled, there were just a few hours left before the wedding was due to start, and Pinx hadn't even begun to think about what the wedding party would wear. Luckily it was a small group. Parrino and Lord Aurelio were soon arrayed in elegant tuxedos, with turquoise ruffled shirts, and fuchsia cummerbunds and bowties. For Lady Cara, Julia's mother, Pinx whipped together a fuchsia chiffon bubble dress, adorned with baublettas and floofle-fluff feathers. She piled the giant's hair high on her head amid a glittering headdress of jangling bangles that twirled like a mobile when she walked.

At last it was time to dress the bride herself, and Pinx spared no effort to make Julia look divine. The white bodice of her wedding gown clung to her body, draping over her shoulders with poofled straps of the sheerest fuchsia glittergloss. The skirt burst out in an explosion of snowy-white fluttereened tulle, and the whole ensemble was festooned with zigzags of glittering beads and glistening gems that snaked over the dress. A tiered headdress held the outfit's crowning gem: a white waterfall veil of white tulle with fuchsia and turquoise piping that cascaded over Julia's perfectly coiffed hair and expertly highlighted features.

The final result? A masterpiece.

While Pinx was working on Julia, she hadn't let the bride see herself in the mirror. Now, when Pinx finally revealed the finished look, Julia stared at her reflection in open-mouthed silence, stunned by her own magnificence.

'Wow,' she gasped eventually. 'If I have to give up all my dreams and throw my life away by marrying a man I don't love . . . at least I'll look beautiful doing it.'

'That's the spirit!' Pinx grinned, and sped off.

By now the wedding was a mere couple of hours away, and Pinx still had to check every detail and put together dazzling makeovers for herself, Silky, Petal, Bizzy and Melody. It seemed beyond impossible that she could get it all done in time. However, as the sun began to set, all five fairies were dressed majestically and ready to welcome all the guests as they strolled in.

If Pinx had any doubts about the effect of

her work, which of course she did not, they were dispelled as soon guests began to arrive. Every giant who entered gaped as their senses were enthralled by the results of Pinx's vision and the fairies' labours. Gorgeous blooms with magnificent aromas covered the grounds and climbed in dazzling colonnades. Fireflies, coaxed by Petal, soared above the affair, blinking their warm glow over everything. Silky's bunting was placed perfectly, creating the sensation that the entire wedding floated in a sea of pastel-coloured clouds. Above it all rang out Melody's magical voice, singing along with the Gigante giant musicians as she floated in front of the altar near the anxious Parrino.

Of course, Pinx felt that the atmosphere would have been even better if every Grande giant didn't have to be searched by Gigante giant soldiers before they entered, or if other Gigante giant soldiers weren't watching the

Grande giant side of the room like hawks, but that was the price for having both giant groups in the same place at the same time.

Bizzy was already crying.

'It's Beyond Blissfully Beautiful!' she sobbed. 'I always Weep Wildly at Weddings.'

'Yes, but at this wedding the bride doesn't want to marry the groom,' Petal reminded her.

'It's still beautiful!' Bizzy insisted, blowing her nose into a handkerchief before bursting into a fresh explosion of sobs.

Silky leaned over to Pinx.

'You're not really planning for Julia to marry Parrino, are you?' she asked.

'It's not up to me,' Pinx said. 'It's up to *him*.'

She nodded her head and Silky followed her gaze to where Romero had just appeared. Gone was the blissfully lovestruck giant the fairies had seen the night before. Romero was white-faced and so sick with grief that he could barely walk. He was leaning heavily on his father, Lord Domino, who led him to a seat beside the aisle.

An impish smile spread across Silky's face.

'You are devious,' she said to Pinx.

'Thank you,' Pinx replied.

Everyone had now arrived, and a hush spread over the guests as the music changed to signal the big moment: the bride walking down the aisle. Everyone shifted in their seats to watch the spectacle – everyone except one Grande giant, whose jaw had dropped at the sound of Melody's voice.

'My bounty is as boundless as the sea, my love as deep; the more I give to thee, the more I have, for both are infinite.'

Melody's enchanting voice sang the beautiful song . . . the same song with which Julia had serenaded Romero only the night before.

'Nice touch,' Silky said to Pinx, who simply raised an eyebrow.

Romero wasn't the only one affected by Pinx's song choice. Julia had appeared at the far end of the aisle, with her parents beside her. Everyone in the room, Grande and Gigante alike, gasped at the sight of her stunning perfection, but Julia could only gape at Melody's song. She scanned the Grande giant side of the room for Romero . . . just as he tore his gaze from Melody to look at Julia.

The two giants' eyes locked, and their love and longing was so clear that the fairies were amazed that every single giant in the room couldn't feel it. Desperately, Romero started to rise to his feet, aching to reach out to Julia, but the Grande giants immediately pulled him back down.

Julia's parents walked her past Romero's row and down the aisle to where Parrino was waiting. Melody finished singing and joined her friends. All the guests were watching the ceremony, but the fairies only had eyes for

Romero. They all understood Pinx's plan, but none of their careful preparations could guarantee that it would work. Now it was all up to Romero.

Finally, the official reached the point in the ceremony for which the fairies were breathlessly waiting.

'If there is anyone here who objects to the union of these two giants, let them speak now or forever hold their peace.'

Holding on to one another in an agony of suspense, Pinx, Silky, Petal, Bizzy and Melody stared breathlessly at Romero. Would he speak? The young giant rose to his feet . . .

'I OBJECT!' boomed a hideous, gravelly voice.

The fairies turned pale with horror as they recognised the owner of the voice.

'No,' cried Melody. 'It can't be!'

'Talon,' Silky confirmed.

The very sound of his name made them all feel ill.

'I OBJECT . . .' the Troll bellowed again, 'ON THE GROUNDS THAT SOME-THING HERE BELONGS TO ME!'

Chapter Ten

The Worst Wedding Crasher

All the wedding guests turned around as Talon the Troll stormed in, his eyes flaring, his teeth bared and his robes floating around him. Here in the Land of Giants, Talon's hulking frame was far from impressive – he was less than half the height of the average Grande or Gigante. Still, he moved as if he were the most fearsome creature anywhere, rampaging down the aisle and flailing his arms to knock down any bunting, flowers or guests' hats that dared stray within reach. At the altar, he stepped between Julia and Parrino and addressed the guests.

'I hate to interrupt the lovely festivities,' he sneered, 'but someone here has a Ring . . . a beautiful Ring, with a centre stone of onyx,

surrounded by diamonds. It's the Ring of Midnight, and it belongs to me. You have exactly one minute to give me this Ring, or I will destroy your entire Land!'

There was a moment of stunned silence. The fairies noticed Lord Aurelio subtly move his left hand over his right, hiding his prized possession from Talon.

Then the room erupted into raucous laughter. Pinx grinned.

'They're *laughing* at him!' she realised. 'This is officially my favourite Land *ever*.'

'Get out of here, little man,' shouted a

giant. 'You're holding up the wedding!'

'"Little man"?' Melody echoed.

She, Petal, Pinx and Bizzy burst out laughing. Silky, however, looked uneasy.

'It's not bothering him,' she said, watching Talon closely. 'He's *smiling*. I don't like it.'

Talon *was* smiling, and his yellowed, rotten grin was more hideous than any scowl imaginable. Then he began to laugh – a mirthless cackle of sound that rattled against every nerve in Silky's body.

'So be it,' Talon announced to the giants. 'You've made your choice . . . now you'll face the consequences.'

Talon closed his eyes and wrapped his arms around his chest. He leaned his head back and started to speak in Trollish. The giants only laughed harder, but Pinx, Petal, Melody and Bizzy's giggles had dried in their throats.

'He's enchanting something,' Melody said worriedly. 'What is it?'

'Giants, please be careful!' Silky cried out to the guests, flying higher so that they could all see her. 'This Troll has magical powers! Please, take cover!'

The giants were laughing too hard to notice Silky, but then a ghastly noise rang out and silenced the giants' mirth. It was a hideous creaking sound, a terrible stretching and snapping and groaning of sinew and bone. It was Talon. And he was growing.

As the giants and fairies gaped in disbelief, Talon's entire body stretched and swelled, taller and wider, until he had grown twice as tall as the largest giant there.

'He enchanted *himself*!' Petal said in disbelief.

But Talon hadn't finished. With another horrific squeal and groan, his body transformed again. Something repulsive rolled and squirmed in his stomach, and Talon cried out for just a moment, bending over double in agony. Then he rose and grinned as a *second Talon* stepped out of the first, this one just as huge and just as terrible.

'Two Titanic Talons?' Bizzy shuddered. 'Too Totally Terrifyingly Terrible.'

'GIVE ME THE RING!' the first Talon roared.

His huge voice shook every chair and rattled every jaw.

'OR SAY GOODBYE TO YOUR LAND!' the second Talon continued.

'Lord Aurelio,' Pinx gasped. 'He doesn't know it's a Talisman. What if he . . .'

She needn't have worried. Like all the giants, Lord Aurelio was too frozen with fear to even think, never mind obey Talon's order.

'FINE!' roared the two oversized Talons in unison.

Each Talon stormed off in an opposite direction, one towards Grande territory, the other towards Gigante territory. Giants leaped away to avoid getting kicked by the Trolls' monstrous feet, but Petal's flower friends weren't so lucky – huge patches were trampled as the Talons stormed off.

Realising that their homes were in danger, the giants snapped out of their stupor.

'Our Land!' cried Lady Cara, Julia's mother. 'Gigantes, stop him!'

'Grandes!' cried Lord Domino. 'We must save our Land! Stop him!'

Every Gigante giant raced off to protect their territory while every Grande sped off in the other direction to protect theirs. Only Lord Aurelio was left at the wedding site, fingering the Ring of Midnight.

It would have been easy to get the Ring from him and fly down the Ladder to safety, but none of the fairies even considered doing that – not with two massive Talons loose in the Land.

Silky thought fast.

'Pinx and Petal, go with the Gigantes and help them fight Talon,' she said. 'Bizzy and I will help fight the Talon on the Grande side. Melody, stay with Lord Aurelio. Explain what's going on, and *do not* let him give the Ring to Talon, no matter what happens!'

On the Gigante side, Pinx and Petal found a nightmare in progress. Not only did this hulking Talon loom over all the giants, but he also had the strength of an army. As Petal watched in horror, he hugged a tree around its middle and ripped it from the ground. With a wicked grin, he wielded the tree like a baseball bat and smashed it into Lord Aurelio's house, reducing a large portion of it to rubble.

'No!' cried Lady Cara.

'Stop him!' Julia screamed.

The Gigante giants tried to stop him, but this monstrous Talon was simply too big and

too strong, and he brushed them off like small children as he continued his rampage of destruction.

'We have to do something!' Pinx shouted to Petal. 'Talk to the plants, the animals . . . can't they help?'

Petal shook her head.

'They're too frightened!' she said. 'It's up to us.'

But Pinx and Petal had no idea how to

stop a Talon so large and powerful.

On the Grande side of the Land, the situation was no better. The Grande giants tried to stop the enormous Talon, but the Troll merely laughed at them. Silky and Bizzy watched as a horde of Grandes ran at Talon. He simply picked one up by the arms and swung the giant around, using him as a weapon to knock over all other giants within reach. Then Talon flung the giant off into the distance.

'Don't let him hit the ground!' Silky cried.

Bizzy quickly magicked up a giant marshmallow to break his fall.

'A marshmallow?' Silky asked.

'It was the first thing I could think of!' Bizzy replied.

But Talon had already moved on to his next attack. He ripped a white fence out of the ground and used the fence posts like spears, throwing them into the crowd of giants. Silky moved quickly and dissolved the most threatening posts with her laser-light, but she knew she couldn't keep it up for very long.

'He's too strong!' Silky wailed to Bizzy. 'We can't stop him! What do we do?'

Chapter Eleven

Grande and Gigante

Step by echoing step, Talon was tracing a massive path of destruction across Gigante giant territory. Wielding his massive bludgeon of a tree, Talon destroyed home after home. The Gigantes, Pinx and Petal were powerless in the face of his immense size and strength.

'It's too much,' Petal admitted. 'We're all too small to stop him.'

It certainly seemed to be true, but everything in Pinx rebelled against the idea. The fairies were incredibly small in this Land – no larger than a giant's pet hamster – and yet they had managed to organise an astoundingly impressive wedding in less than twenty-four hours, just by working together.

'That's it!' Pinx cried. 'Petal, I know the animals are scared, but I need them to help us to get the Gigantes' attention. They won't be in any danger, I promise.'

Pinx explained what she needed, and Petal understood. She closed her eyes and concentrated, calling out to every animal she could reach, asking desperately for their help.

Moments later, every dog, cat, squirrel, raccoon and bird in the area streamed out of the houses and trees in Gigante territory and surrounded the Gigante giants, herding them away from Talon. The Gigantes were incredibly confused by the animals' behaviour, and allowed themselves to be gathered in a large circle, over which Pinx soared.

'Everyone, I need your attention!' Pinx shouted. 'You cannot defeat Talon on your own. If you want to succeed, you need to go to Grande territory and work *with* the Grandes to defeat the Talon over there!'

A murmur of disbelief spread through the crowd.

'Why should we save their Land and let ours be destroyed?' demanded one giant.

'This Land belongs to all of you,' Petal declared.

'Besides, you won't be letting this Land be destroyed,' Pinx added. 'Talon may have split in two, but he's still one Troll. Work together to defeat one of him and you'll defeat them both. But if you stay apart, the Grandes and Gigantes will both fail; only Talon will win.'

There was a moment's silence as the Gigantes considered this. Then the distant crunch of another house being destroyed snapped them out of their reverie.

'Let's do it!' cried Julia. 'Let's join the Grandes and save our Land!'

Realising that it was their only option for success, the Gigantes roared their approval and raced towards Grande territory.

In Grande territory itself, things had got even worse. There too, Talon was using a huge tree like a bat, smashing it into house after house. However, the din of destruction was almost drowned out as the horde of roaring Gigante giants approached.

'Lord Domino!' Julia cried. 'We're here to help! Tell us what we can do!'

Lord Domino stopped in his tracks, surprised by this offer of help from his enemy. Then he heard another house crunch, and he snapped back into action.

'Yes!' he cried. 'We'll work together! After him!'

As the giants swarmed towards Talon, Pinx and Petal joined Silky and Bizzy.

'You got the Gigantes to come and help the Grandes?' Silky asked in amazement. 'You're a genius!'

Silky hugged Pinx and the fairies set off to join the giants in battle. Suddenly they were interrupted by a hideously loud roar of fury.

'YOU THINK YOU CAN GET AWAY THAT EASILY?' roared the *other* Talon.

He had come to Grande territory when he realised that the Gigante giants were no longer paying attention to him. Pinx quickly took charge of the situation.

'Keep working together!' she told the giants. 'Leave this Talon to us!'

'TO *YOU*?' laughed the monstrous Talon closest the fairies. 'YOU'RE MINUSCULE COMPARED TO ME! YOU CAN DO NOTHING!'

He swiped at the fairies with an enormous hand and sent them scattering for cover.

'We just have to distract him,' Pinx whispered to her friends as they hurried back together. 'The giants can take care of the other one.'

The fairies leaped into action. Silky flashed a beam of laser-light at a tree, breaking off a branch that smacked on to Talon's head.

'OW!' Talon roared.

'Silky!' Petal gasped.

'What?' Silky exclaimed. 'I had to do *something*!'

'Trees are our friends!' Petal insisted. 'You don't have to hurt them to get their help!'

As Talon staggered under the blow from the branch, Petal called out to a nearby flowering tree, which rained pollen on to the Troll, making him sneeze uncontrollably.

'See?' Petal asked, turning her back on Talon to look at Silky.

Talon stopped sneezing and reached out to grab Petal.

'Oh no you don't!' Bizzy cried.

She pushed Petal aside and muttered a magical spell that made a rotten egg appear in Petal's place. It fell on Talon, splattering all over him.

'UGH!' Talon wailed, gagging at the

nauseating smell.

He wiped the disgusting egg ooze on his cloak ('Gaggingly Gross!' Bizzy moaned), and then came after the fairies yet again. This time, Pinx was ready. She had spotted a long rug in the hall of a house whose wall Talon had smashed, and flew full speed towards Talon, the rug trailing behind her like a kite tail. She zipped around and around Talon's head, wrapping it in the rug and blindfolding him.

Talon stumbled around blindly as he tried to remove the rug, and when he succeeded he was angrier than ever. He lunged for Pinx and was about to grab her when an impossibly shrill screech sounded in his ear, making him stagger back in pain. Melody had flown up and sung the high note directly into his ear canal.

'I heard what was going on and I couldn't stay away,' Melody said. 'And neither could he.'

She gestured towards Lord Aurelio, who was racing to join the other giants. While Talon had been able to handle an onslaught from half the Land of Giants, the entire population was too much. Every time he threw aside one giant, another was there to take his or her place. Giants climbed on top of him, battering his head, back and chest. Giants clung on to his legs and arms, weighing him down so that he couldn't move. Others tied the motionless Talon's shoelaces together. Then they let go of the Troll, giving him the freedom to move . . . and trip over his tied-together shoes.

As soon as Talon hit the ground, a crowd of giants swarmed over him, while others rushed into nearby houses to fetch ropes, belts and curtain ties . . . anything that could be used to tie him down. Lord Aurelio and Lord Domino worked together to tie the final knot that secured Talon, who was now mummy-like and helpless. Talon saw the Ring on Lord Aurelio's finger and his eyes grew wide as he tried to free himself. But he was trussed up tightly and he couldn't move.

At that moment the other Talon recovered from Melody's brain-scrambling screech. He lunged at the fairies, and then stopped in his tracks as if he had been paralysed.

'NO!' cried both Talons in unison.

The standing Talon faded away into nothingness. As Pinx had suspected, the two Talons were still just one Troll: when one had been stopped, the other could no longer exist. The enchantment was broken, and the remaining Talon began to return to his usual size. The ropes that bound him fell away as he shrank.

'Tie him again!' Lord Aurelio cried in alarm.

The giants quickly re-tied Talon, but they

needn't have worried.

'Look at him,' Petal told the other fairies. 'He's so weak that he can't even move.'

It was true. The effort of enchanting himself had drained Talon completely. He was weak and pale, and didn't even complain when a Grande giant hoisted him over his shoulder to carry him away.

'Wait!' Silky cried, flying after the giant who held Talon. 'I want his crystal necklace. It's time we delivered it back to Witch Whisper.'

She reached for the necklace, but it was no longer around Talon's neck.

'It's gone!' Silky exclaimed. 'It's the source of his magic; he'd never let it go. He must have hidden it somewhere.'

'If he has, we'll find it,' Lord Domino assured Silky. 'He won't cause any more trouble with it, I promise you.'

Lord Domino nodded to the Grande giant who held Talon, and the giant took Talon off to his new home: a Grande giant prison cell. Lord Domino turned to Lord Aurelio.

'It seems I owe you an apology, Lord Aurelio,' he said. 'Without you and the Gigante giants, we Grandes would have lost everything.'

'Without you and the Grandes, we would have lost everything as well,' Lord Aurelio agreed. 'Perhaps . . . perhaps we've misjudged one another all this time.'

'Perhaps we have,' echoed Lord Domino.

The two giants grasped hands and smiled, and then everyone erupted into cheers and applause . . . everyone except Bizzy, who burst into tears.

'Bizzy, why are you crying?' asked Melody. 'This is wonderful!'

'I know!' sobbed Bizzy. 'But I always cry at the end of Fiercely Fought Feuds. Those and weddings.'

'Weddings!' cried Pinx. 'What better way to

celebrate a new beginning than with a wedding! Right, Julia?'

Pinx looked meaningfully at Julia, and the giant nodded. She took a deep breath and turned to the crowd.

'I agree,' she said, 'and I invite everyone here to witness my wedding . . .' She strode to Romero and took his hand in hers, '. . . to Romero: a Grande giant and the love of my life.'

The fairies held their breath. The two groups seemed to have ended their feud, but would they actually accept a marriage between Grande and Gigante?

Chapter Twelve

Happily Ever After

'Do you take this man to be your lawfully wedded husband?'

'I do,' replied Julia.

'Do you take this woman to be your lawfully wedded wife?'

'I do,' beamed Romero.

'Then by the power vested in me, I now pronounce you husband and wife. You may kiss the bride.'

Romero and Julia leaned towards one another and shared a kiss so full of love that everyone who witnessed it burst into spontaneous cheers and applause. But no one cheered as loudly as Petal, Melody, Bizzy, Silky and Pinx.

In the end, after everything they'd been

through, only Parrino had been truly upset by Julia's announcement that she wanted to marry Romero. But even he gave up Julia's hand gracefully when he saw the depth of the love that the two giants shared.

There were many things that had needed to be done before the giants could really enjoy a wedding. The Land was in a shambles after Talon's attack. Bizzy had used her magic to mend the ruined Grande and Gigante homes (accidentally adding the occasional bonus, like replacing a simple *wall* with a giant *banquet hall*, or replacing a delighted child's ruined *bookmark* with a fully functioning *amusement park*). Meanwhile, the other fairies had worked hard to return the wedding area to its original splendour.

After the wedding, Lord Aurelio fulfilled his promise to his daughter and gave her the Ring of Midnight, which she immediately presented to the fairies.

'I'll never forget you,' Julia said. 'And I can't thank you enough for all you've done for me. For all of us.'

'Just love each other and be happy,' Pinx said with a smile. 'That's all the thanks we need.' She thought for a second, and then added, 'And maybe a staggeringly brilliant write-up in your best fashion magazine. You know, for my scrapbook.'

'Done,' Julia promised.

The fairies said goodbye and sped off towards the Ladder, holding on to the Ring and supporting its massive weight between them.

Back in the Faraway Tree, the fairies were thrilled to be able safely to deliver the Land of Giants' Talisman to Witch Whisper, who returned it to the Vault. The fairies were eager to visit Gino and tell him the truth about the Gigante giants, but that would have to wait. Right now they needed to sleep.

As the five friends happily soared up the Tree to their home, Bizzy couldn't stop grinning at Pinx.

'What?' Pinx finally exploded.

'Nothing,' retorted Bizzy. 'It's just . . . you're a Super-Secret Softy!'

'Oh stop it,' Pinx said, smiling.

'Bizzy's right,' Petal said. 'We didn't have to

get involved with Julia and Romero. That came from you . . . and it changed everything.'

'Yes, well,' said Pinx, 'I just can't stand to see a girl forced into a life she doesn't want.'

Silky looked curiously at Pinx. Was there some kind of story behind that? Pinx gave nothing away, but just kept flying straight ahead. Silky decided not to press her. If there *was* a story behind it, there was plenty of time to find out. Instead she just smiled.

'I'm not sure what we would have done

without you up there,' Silky told Pinx. 'You were pretty amazing.'

'Of course I was,' Pinx said flippantly.

But she turned and met Silky's eyes, and it was clear that Silky's compliment had touched her.

'But that's just because I had you lot with me all the way,' Pinx added in earnest. 'We're quite a team.'

'The *best* team,' Melody agreed.

'A Particularly Perfect Panoply of Personalities,' Bizzy chimed in.

'Where do you think we'll go next?' Petal asked.

'Ugh – I don't even want to think about it right now!' Silky cried. 'No more adventure talk until we've had some sleep – deal?'

The others all laughed and agreed. But in her head, Pinx *was* thinking about the next adventure. She was picturing the moment when Witch Whisper and Cluecatcher would again appear at their house, and she was anticipating the excitement she would feel, knowing in her heart that she could be there for her friends as much as they were always there for her.

If you can't wait for another exciting adventure with Silky and her fairy friends, here's a sneak preview . . .

Chapter One

Panic at the Party

How had Bizzy ever let Pinx talk her into this? From her room high in the fairies' treehouse, Bizzy looked down at the crowd and gasped. Nearly every single resident of the Faraway Tree was jammed into the main room, and their excited chatter blended into a wordless, ebbing and flowing roar, like the sound of ocean waves crashing on to the beach. Bizzy felt a little seasick.

The party had originally been Bizzy's idea. It had been a few months since the fairies moved to the Faraway Tree, and Bizzy thought it would be tremendous fun to have a celebration in the treehouse. Pinx had loved the idea and taken over the organisation, transforming the fun little party into a magnificent gala of epic proportions. She had decided that Melody would be in charge of music, Silky would handle the lighting, Petal would decorate and Bizzy . . .

'You can use your magic to create the party theme!' Pinx had exclaimed.

'What do you mean?' Bizzy had asked.

'The best parties have themes,' Pinx had enthused. 'Like "Under the Sea" or "Over the Rainbow" or . . .' Pinx gasped and her eyes grew wide, '. . . "*Among the Stars*"! Yes! And with your magic you can actually make it seem as if the treehouse is in outer space! You can make shooting stars, and swirling galaxies, and . . . and no gravity! We won't just dance at this party; we'll *float*! It'll be the most incredible thing the Faraway Tree has ever seen!'

Bizzy could only gape as Pinx went on and on. Turn the treehouse into outer space? Turn off gravity? Bizzy knew that she had the magical skills to do it, but her record wasn't exactly perfect when it came to making her spells work. Bizzy was sure that one way or another, this would turn into a terrible mess.

'I don't know, Pinx,' she said. 'Maybe I could just make snacks for the party. I'm Fantastically Famous For Fantabulous Food!'

'That's a great idea!' Pinx agreed.

Bizzy relaxed . . . almost.

'So it's settled then,' Pinx continued. 'You're in charge of food and theming.'

'But –' Bizzy began to object.

'Can't talk – got to spread the word!' Pinx said, and flew off.

Between then and the party, Bizzy had tried about a million times to explain to Pinx that counting on her to turn the party into a Grand Galactic Gala was a *bad* idea. Unfortunately, Pinx seemed only to hear the words 'Grand Galactic Gala', which was how she described the party to every single creature in the Tree . . . all of whom were now inside the treehouse. They talked, they danced, they munched on Bizzy-baked delights like Crackle Corn, Gigglybeans and Goo-drops . . . but mostly, Bizzy knew, they were waiting for Bizzy to reveal her incredible theme.

Pinx soared high above everyone's heads. It was time for Bizzy's 'grand entrance' – another Pinx idea, and the reason why Bizzy was tucked away in her room. Melody stopped the music and Silky concentrated a spotlight on Pinx. Everyone looked up expectantly.

'Faraway Tree friends!' Pinx cried. 'It is now my great pleasure to present Bizzy, who will turn this party into a Grand Galactic Gala!'

'HURRAY!' cheered the crowd.

Pinx flew up to Bizzy's room and escorted her out. The crowd roared even louder when Bizzy appeared. Witch Whisper, Cluecatcher, Gino, Dame Washalot, Moonface, Saucepan

Man, Elf Cloudshine, Zuni, Misty . . . even the Eternal Bloom had been moved out of her spot in Petal's garden to be part of the excitement. They were all crowded together, pressed shoulder to shoulder amidst the towering branches of the tree. Of course Bizzy's best friends were there as well – Silky, Petal, Melody and Pinx – all smiling at her, waiting for her to do exactly what Pinx had promised. Bizzy really didn't want to let them down. She took a deep breath.

'Here goes nothing,' she said to herself.

She caught Silky's eye, and Silky nodded, assuring Bizzy that it would be fine, that she could do this. Bizzy hoped that her friend was right. She raised her arms high, then spoke the spells that would turn the room into a zero-gravity fantasy land, filled with shooting stars.

'Gravitateraminous, whizzeeo-starreeo-zoomerangle-swooshlesticks!'

Bizzy plunged ten feet towards the ground.

Below her, every guest dropped to the floor with a loud thump.

'What's going on?' wailed Moonface. 'I can't stand up!'

Bizzy hadn't got rid of gravity; she had made it *stronger*! Every move felt like swimming through treacle.

Then came the shooting stars. At least, they were supposed to be shooting stars, but Bizzy got the spell just a little bit mixed up and made shooting *bars*. Chocolate bars, to be specific, in every possible flavour. They filled the air, zipping and zooming in all directions.

'AAAHHH!' Bizzy cried, dodging to avoid a toffee bar that was heading straight for her face.

This was horrible. Just as she had feared, she had turned the gala into one big mess. But Silky, Melody and Petal didn't seem angry at all, and in fact laughed delightedly as they plucked their favourite chocolate treats from the sky.

'This is so silly!' giggled Melody, as she tumbled forwards to intercept a particularly yummy-looking chocolate-covered marshmallow bar.

'It's not supposed to be silly, it's supposed to be spectacular!' Pinx retorted, ducking away from a spear of chocolate crisp.

The crisp continued on its way to Petal, who happily grabbed it and took a giant bite.

'It *is*,' Petal noted. 'It's *spectacularly* silly.'

Silky swallowed her mouthful of malted milk bar and curled in her wings to avoid a passing buttercream.

'Exactly!' she added. 'And everyone loves it . . . except for the Angry Pixie, of course.'

They all looked down. While most of the gravity-slowed crowd was emulating the fairies and delighting in the torrents of sweets, the Angry Pixie was screaming as he flailed flat on his back.

'I'm stuck!' he shouted.

A flurry of caramel bars had crashed into him, and the gooey insides had left him pasted to the floor.

'I demand that this party stops right now!' he wailed.

As he opened his mouth to complain again, some of the caramel dripped into it. Tasting the sweet, melting treat, the Angry Pixie paused and then grinned.

'I'm absolutely scrumptious!' he cried, and quickly stopped wailing and started licking the delicious caramel off his face.

Pinx laughed. Perhaps the party was a success after all. Bizzy, however, was still a bit upset that she hadn't been able to give everyone what they had been promised.

'Look at Cluecatcher!' Melody giggled. 'I never knew he liked chocolate bars so much.'

The fairies followed Melody's gaze. All eight of Cluecatcher's eyes were staring intently at the ceiling. As the chocolate bars whizzed his way, he spun his radar-dish ears around and around, collecting sweets with every turn. Then he leaned back until his huge nostrils pointed straight to the sky and gave a mighty sniff. . . vacuuming piles of chocolate bars towards his face. Four of the fairies laughed, but Silky suspected that something other than a sweet tooth was behind Cluecatcher's actions.

'A new Land is coming to the top of the Tree!' Cluecatcher cried.

Immediately, Witch Whisper's voice boomed through the room.

'I am sorry, everyone, but this party is over!' she announced.

With a quick spell and a wave of her arm, she undid Bizzy's magic, banishing the flying chocolates and returning gravity to normal. As everyone started to file out, happily munching on the last of their sweets, the fairies and Witch Whisper surrounded Cluecatcher. His eyes still trained on the ceiling, Cluecatcher gave a mighty sniff. He held in the breath, rolling it around in his mouth as the fairies leaned in closer and closer, waiting with excitement to hear which land was coming to the Faraway Tree. Finally he breathed out a long, slow breath, turned to the fairies and smiled.

'Sleepover Land!' he announced.

'Sleepover Land,' Witch Whisper repeated, 'where every day is a sleepover.'

'Every day?' Bizzy asked, her eyes wide with awe.

The excitement of a new Land completely crowded out her disappointment about the party.

'Every day,' replied Witch Whisper. 'The Land's Talisman is the Bedtime Bear: the ultimate stuffed toy. Its embrace gives the gift of peaceful slumber to anyone who wishes for it. You should go now; we don't know how long the Land will be at the top of the Tree.'

'Yes! Let's go now!' Melody cried. 'I love sleepovers!'

'Then I expect you'll have an interesting time,' said Witch Whisper with a smile. 'I only hope that you remain focused and can return safely with the Talisman. And please be careful of Talon; I know you left him locked away in the Land of Giants, but he is strong and clever. If he has found a way out, he'll be after the Bedtime Bear . . . and all of you.'

The fairies promised that they would be careful and then soared out of their treehouse to the Ladder. Despite Witch Whisper's warning, they were thrilled to start their mission. After all, what could possibly be more exciting than a Land where every day is a sleepover?